"An intelligent and thought-provoking drama that casts a less-than-glowing light on man's dark side in the face of disaster . . . The play's energy lies in LaBute's trademark scathing dialogue."
—Robert Dominguez, New York *Daily News*

"Though set in the cold, gray light of morning in a downtown loft with inescapable views of the vacuum left by the twin towers, *The Mercy Seat* really occurs in one·of those feverish nights of the soul in which men and women lock in vicious sexual combat, as in Strindberg's *Dance of Death* and Edward Albee's *Who's Afraid of Virginia Woolf?*"   —Ben Brantley, *The New York Times*

"[A] powerful drama . . . LaBute shows a true master's hand in gliding us amid the shoals and reefs of a mined relationship."
—Donald Lyons, *New York Post*

"Uncomfortable yet fascinating . . . *The Mercy Seat* makes for provocative theater—sharp, compelling and more than a little chilling."   —Michael Kuchwara, *Newsday*

"LaBute's intriguing . . . new play . . . is most compelling when it is daring to look into [a] character's heart to explore the way self-interest, given the opportunity, can swamp all our nobler instincts."   —Charles Isherwood, *Variety*

"In *The Mercy Seat* . . . LaBute has given us his most compelling portrait of male inner turmoil."
—Brendan Lemon, *The Financial Times*

"LaBute [is] the dark shining star of stage and film morality."

—Linda Winer, *Newsday*

"The sharply funny and incisive *Seat* is not a response to September 11, but a response to the response to September 11—an emotionally jarring consideration of the self-serving exploitation of tragedy for personal gain . . . Perhaps it's time we stop thinking of LaBute as a mere provocateur, a label that condescends to an artist of grand ambition and a nimble facility with language. With this gripping . . . new drama, he probes deeper than he ever has before."　　　　—Jason Zinoman, *TimeOut New York*

"A nihilistic yet brutally honest work . . . as complex and unfathomable as human motivations . . . *The Mercy Seat* is haunting."

—David A. Rosenberg, *Backstage*

"LaBute risks offending contemporary sensibilities by using a historic tragedy as his turning point for a drama regarding a morally empty American . . . [*The Mercy Seat* is] controversial and compelling."　　　　—Michael Sommers, *The Star-Ledger*

"LaBute . . . is holding up a pitiless mirror to ourselves. We may not like what we see, but we can't deny that—if only in some dark corner of our souls—it is there."

—Jacques le Sourd, *The Journal News*

NEIL LABUTE

The Mercy Seat

Neil LaBute is a critically acclaimed writer-director for both the stage and the screen. His controversial and much discussed works include the plays *The Distance from Here* and *bash: latterday plays*; and the films *In the Company of Men* (Faber, 1997), *Your Friends and Neighbors* (Faber, 1998), *Nurse Betty*, and *Possession*; as well as the play and film adaptation of *The Shape of Things* (Faber, 2001).

Also by Neil LaBute

In the Company of Men
Your Friends and Neighbors
The Shape of Things

The Mercy Seat

The Mercy Seat

Seat

A PLAY BY

Neil LaBute

FABER AND FABER

New York / London

FABER AND FABER, INC.
An affiliate of Farrar, Straus and Giroux
18 West 18th Street, New York 10011

Faber and Faber Ltd
3 Queen Square
London WC1N 3AU

Library of Congress Control Number: 2002114016
ISBN-13: 978-0-571-21138-8
ISBN-10: 0-571-21138-0

Designed by Gretchen Achilles

www.fsgbooks.com

15   14

For David Hare

Approach, my soul, the mercy-seat,
Where Jesus answers prayers;
There humbly fall before his feet,
For none can perish there.

—STANDARD CHURCH HYMN

A wind with a wolf's head
Howled about our door,
And we burned up the chairs
And sat upon the floor.

—EDNA ST. VINCENT MILLAY

And the mercy seat is waiting
And I think my head is burning
And in a way I'm yearning
To be done with all this measuring of truth.

—NICK CAVE

Preface

I have no idea why I wrote this play. Really, I don't.

In March of 2002, I found myself sitting on a plane bound for somewhere, pretty much minding my own business, and the idea struck me. This notion—something about what a person would really do if they were afforded the chance to wipe the slate clean and start life over—simply came to me and I followed it to its illogical conclusion. I say "illogical" because the story of *The Mercy Seat* is anything but expected. September 11, 2001, saw to that. And while I don't think of this piece as a significant response to the attack, the particulars of the plot mechanics could have been put into motion only by the catastrophic events of that notorious Tuesday. When the thought came to me, I did what I always do: I chased after the muse and wrestled her to the ground. (In reality, I pulled out my laptop, ordered a ginger ale, and got to work.)

The destruction of two buildings in New York City and the un-fathomable loss of life that followed hangs like a damaged umbrella over the events of *The Mercy Seat.* Yet it is not a play that concerns itself with the politics of terrorism. Perhaps it does, actually, but it is a particular kind of terrorism: the painful, simplistic warfare we often wage on the hearts of those we profess to love. Above all else, this play is a "relationship" play, in the purest sense. It is well made (as the French used to say) if not well-meaning. It is also written in a way that I am fairly unused to. Its characters have first and last names. It takes place in a single long act in one location. It unfolds in a named city on a specific day. The work itself fairly spilled out of me and onto the page. It came in harsh, sorrowful bursts and wouldn't stop, not just because of that day, that damned day in September, but because I could also see something of myself on the page. And the guy who was sitting across the aisle from me. And the woman in the security line. And you, probably, you there holding this book in your hands. In *The Mercy Seat* I am trying to examine the "ground zero" of our lives, that gaping hole in ourselves that we try to cover up with clothes from The Gap, with cologne from Ralph Lauren, with handbags from Kate Spade. Why are we willing to run a hundred miles around simply saying to someone, "I don't know if I love you anymore"? Why? Because Nikes are cheap, running is easy, and honesty is the hardest, coldest currency on the planet.

My work, until this point, has tended to exist in a geographic and moral vacuum. Now I have written a play about two New Yorkers who face down one another and their own selves on a long, dark morning of the soul. I hold the mirror up higher and try to examine how selfishness can still exist during a moment of national selflessness. I don't know exactly why I put fingers to keyboard on this one, but here it is. Like any other play I've written, it came both easily and with difficulty. It was rewarding and painful to be a part of. I love it and I hate it. It is what it is. So be it.

—NEIL LABUTE

October 18, 2002

The Mercy Seat

Production History

The Mercy Seat had its world premiere on November 26, 2002, at the Manhattan Class Company (MCC) Theater in New York City. Director: Neil LaBute. Artistic Directors: Robert LuPone and Bernard Telsey. Associate Artistic Director: William Cantler. Set design: Neil Patel; costume design: Catherine Zuber; lighting design: James Vermeulen; original music and sound design: David Van Tieghem. Production Stage Manager: Stacy P. Hughes. Production Manager: B.D. White. Press Representative: Boneau/ Bryan-Brown. Casting: Bernard Telsey Casting.

The cast was as follows:

BEN HARCOURT   Liev Schreiber

ABBY PRESCOTT   Sigourney Weaver

Characters

BEN HARCOURT   male, thirties
ABBY PRESCOTT   female, forties

Setting

New York City, not long ago

NOTE: A / denotes a suggested point of overlap between that line and the next actor's line.

Silence. Darkness.

A spacious loft apartment, well appointed. Doors leading off in several directions, suggesting a hallway to bedrooms and a bathroom or two. A stainless-steel kitchen, visible. Three large arched windows display a view of other buildings across the street. A kind of amber haze in the air.

This is a large sitting room with lovely couches and chairs. Bookshelves heaped high. Framed pictures. A television plays quietly in one corner. A layer of white dust on everything. Absolutely everything.

BEN, *maybe thirty-three, sits pressed into the corner of one loveseat, staring straight ahead. A cell phone rests in one hand. It rings and rings.*

After a long moment, the front door opens and a woman of about forty-five enters, also covered in dust and carrying several plastic bags. This is ABBY. *She sees* BEN *as she removes an Hermès scarf from around her mouth, but she says nothing, continuing on to the kitchen. She takes off her coat and hat, then begins putting groceries away. When she can't stand it any longer, she walks over and takes the phone out of his hand and pushes a button. The ringing stops and she returns the phone to* BEN. *White clouds of dust follow her every move.*

ABBY Save it.
BEN Hmm?

ABBY The phone. I turned it off to save it.

BEN That's okay.

ABBY I know it's okay, I know that. That's why I did it, because it's okay.

BEN Right. / Sure.

ABBY If you're not going to use it, then you should keep it off. / Save the battery.

BEN Uh-huh.

ABBY Plus the sound . . . drives me crazy. You know?

BEN Sorry . . . I didn't hear it.

ABBY Oh. *(She laughs.)* Okay . . . *(She stands over* BEN *until he finally looks up. Doesn't say anything else. She shakes her head and moves back to the kitchen.)* So . . . did you call?

BEN Huh?

ABBY "Call." I asked if you called.

BEN Ummm . . .

ABBY Of course you didn't. I know you didn't.

BEN No, I didn't.

ABBY I knew it.

BEN Didn't answer it, either . . .

ABBY And are you planning to?

BEN I'm . . . I was, ahh . . . I was going to, maybe . . .

ABBY Yeah, that's pretty much where I left you. At the "babbling-to-myself" stage.

BEN I keep trying to.

ABBY Really?

BEN Yeah, but . . . but I'm . . .

ABBY Huh. *(She walks over again, billowing little clouds of white*

Neil LaBute

behind her. She takes back the phone for a moment, turns it on. Waits. Checks something as it begins ringing almost immediately.) The last number you called was the Chinese place. Yesterday morning, for your shirts. *I* called, actually . . . remember?

BEN Yes. / I do.

ABBY Good. / Just so we're on the same page here . . . *(Looking at the display.)* It's for *you. (She sighs and turns the phone off in mid-ring. Hands it back.)*

BEN What I meant was . . . in my head, I was trying to . . . Several times. But I . . .

ABBY You couldn't. Right? / Just *couldn't* do it . . .

BEN No. I guess not. / No.

ABBY So, you want to, then? You haven't, but you want to . . .

BEN I dunno. I guess so . . . shouldn't I?

ABBY Oh, I can't help you with this one. Uh-uh . . . *This* one's all up to you.

BEN I know, I know . . . I just . . .

ABBY You should, of course. Call.

BEN Yes.

ABBY I mean, it's the decent thing to do.

BEN That's true . . .

ABBY It's the *only* thing to do, really . . .

BEN Uh-huh.

ABBY You know that, right?

BEN Yeah. *(Beat.)* Yeah, I do . . . Yes.

ABBY Yeah. *(Beat.)* Funny thing is, you were going to, anyway. I mean, for a *different* reason, obviously, but that's what you said.

BEN I did. / I did say that . . .

ABBY That's what you told me. / You said, "I'm going to call her. I am. Right now." You were sitting on that couch, the same *spot*, really, and I was kneeling between your legs when you told me that. Five minutes before it happened. Like, a *minute* before all this . . . happened. *(Beat.)* Of course, we've heard about that one a few times now, haven't we? The BIG CALL.

BEN Yes.

ABBY Yeah, just a couple. / "I'm going to do it, I promise. This time I mean it." *(Beat.)* I even threw in a little incentive, didn't I? / Down there on my hands and knees . . .

BEN I'm aware of that. / Yes. / I did say it, I know . . . and I should. Call.

ABBY But that doesn't really mean shit. Does it?

BEN I guess not.

ABBY That's what I like about you, Ben. Your absolutely rigid commitment to being a flake.

BEN Thanks.

ABBY You're welcome.

BEN A lot.

ABBY You're welcome a lot. *(Beat.)* You want a snack? It's cheese.

BEN No thanks, but . . . no.

ABBY I'm gonna have some. I'm going to have some cheese.

BEN That's all right.

ABBY I know it is! I know it's all right, and that's why I'm going to have some. I'm going to fix myself a plate of this nice

Havarti that I bought for you and a few crackers, and then I'm
... I'm going to ...

BEN Go ahead.

ABBY Oh, I will, I will ... I'm ... I think I'll just ... I'll ... *(She
doesn't finish the sentence but just nods to herself. She goes
to the kitchen and begins to cut into the fleshy white cheese
and then stops as the tears come. She puts her head down,
but her shoulders betray her. After a moment, she calms herself and looks over at* BEN, *who hasn't moved but is looking at
her.)* That was a test, by the way ... to see if you have a decent fucking bone in your body. / Which you failed.

BEN I just ... / I'm sorry, Abby, but ...

ABBY What? You what ... ? Tell me.

BEN I just can't right now.

ABBY "Can't?"

BEN No ... not at the moment.

ABBY "Can't" what? Be human?!

BEN No. I can't, no. / Not at this time.

ABBY Jesus, you're amazing ... / Seriously, you are.

BEN I'm just telling you how it is ...

ABBY Oh great. Thanks, Ben, thanks a *bunch.*

ABBY *takes a piece of cheese and shoves it in her mouth.
Chews.* BEN *sits up a bit, brushes off his legs. He turns on the
phone and looks at it. It rings.*

BEN Should I ... ?

ABBY Answer it or keep it off. It's up to you.

BEN Maybe I should . . . I mean . . .

ABBY Yeah, maybe you really, really should. Go ahead.

BEN . . . just say I'm doing all right or . . . / You know . . .

ABBY Go ahead. / Do it.

BEN Yeah . . . I probably should.

ABBY An-swer! *(Just then the phone stops ringing. Dead quiet. Maybe the sound of sirens way off.)* Too late. You're too late, Ben. As always.

BEN I see that.

ABBY Once again, your ability to be completely off the mark is uncanny.

BEN Thanks, honey.

ABBY Fuck. You.

BEN Thanks again.

ABBY Welcome. *(They look at each other and almost smile. Almost.* BEN *fiddles with his cell phone a bit while* ABBY *nibbles at a cracker.)* It's been nearly a day . . .

BEN I know.

ABBY Almost an entire day since it happened.

BEN I know that.

ABBY I mean, the world has gone absolutely *nuts* out there; it really, really has . . . No idea what's happening, no one does, the army patrolling around—there are people in *camouflage* on the Brooklyn Bridge—and you're, I don't know, just . . . I don't know where you are.

BEN Abby, I'm right here.

ABBY Why is that not comforting when you say it?

BEN I . . . I'm just saying that I know what's happening. I do. I'm aware of the situation here. / And out there . . .

ABBY You are? / Really?

BEN Yeah, really. Yes . . .

ABBY Huh. *(Beat.)* And all that knowledge of yours . . . it doesn't make you wanna do something? I mean, not even just a little bit?

BEN Of course . . . yeah, of course it does. But . . .

ABBY Ahh, "but." There's always a "but" when you talk to Ben Harcourt.

BEN Abby, that's not . . .

ABBY "I'd love to, but . . ." "This Friday would be great, but . . ."

BEN Stop.

ABBY "Sure, you can suck my dick, but . . ."

BEN Abby, STOP IT!

ABBY Why don't you just change your name? It's only two letters and you're there. "B-U-T" instead of "B-E-N." / It's not a bad little nickname . . .

BEN Abby, I said . . . / Why are you doing this?

ABBY Because it makes me curious, that's all. *(Beat.)* When I was out there, walking around, staring at people . . . I suddenly wondered how you feel about it. I mean, *really* feel about what's happened.

BEN I feel like everybody else does. / I do!

ABBY I don't think that's true. / No, uh-uh. *(Beat.)* 'Cause after the shock of it, okay, after the obvious sort of shock that anyone goes through . . . your first thought was that this is an opportunity . . .

BEN Yeah, but I meant . . . for us. / Just as a *possibility* for *us* . . .

ABBY Who does that?! / Who in their right mind is going to see . . . *this* . . . as having "unlimited potential"?

BEN I didn't mean it like . . . / No, I just meant that . . .

ABBY It's a meal ticket, that's exactly what you said! / "Our meal ticket" to a banquet that, lately, you haven't seemed all that eager to attend . . . / Meaning, "me."

BEN Abby, that's not . . . / No, that is not the . . .

ABBY And so that's why I'm wondering, I just wanna know . . . how does Mr. Ben Harcourt feel inside about all this? Hmm?

BEN I feel . . . you know . . . / I'm very . . . I mean . . .

ABBY No, Ben, I don't know. That's why I'm asking you. / How do *you* feel? Hmm?

BEN Not good.

ABBY "Not good." Well, that's succinct, anyway.

BEN I do! I feel . . . It's awful. I mean, my God. I can't even . . .

ABBY Sure, you can. Go on.

BEN What do you want me to say, Abby? Jesus. *(Beat.)* It's horrific. A complete and, and, and utter . . .

ABBY Fill in the blank.

BEN . . . tragedy. It's beyond belief. Biblical.

ABBY Jesus, you sound like *Dan Rather.*

BEN Hey, I'm a little . . . / Oh yeah, it's so goddamn easy to . . .

ABBY You left out "calamity" and "moral abyss." / Tell me how it makes you *feel!*

BEN Shitty, okay?! I feel shitty about it!!

ABBY And why's that?

BEN You know why . . . / Come off it . . .

ABBY No, I don't, no . . . not really. / No, we talked about "thank God you weren't in there" and other survivor guilt–type shit, but we haven't really discussed how you . . .

BEN Jesus, Abby, this is . . . what do you want? I can't believe it!

I'm in shock. I feel like I'm gonna throw up, okay, like I might just heave my guts out here on your . . . faux-Persian rug or something. How's that? I-feel-shitty! Is that enough?

ABBY It's a start. *(Beat.)* The rug's real, by the way.

BEN I don't know what to say.

ABBY Well, that's nothing new. *(Beat.)* So . . . how shitty?

BEN Abby!

ABBY No, I just mean "shitty" enough to walk out and do something about it? To go pitch in down at a hospital, or hand out food . . . On a shitty scale of 1 to 10, how shitty is your shitty feeling?

BEN You're just trying to provoke something here.

ABBY No, I'm not at all. I'm really interested. I am. *(Beat.)* I was thinking about this last night, woke up next to you on the couch there and I started thinking. I mean, I know how *I* feel, I know that, and I just wanted to be clear about where you and I stand on this thing. As a couple, I mean.

BEN What "thing"?

ABBY Just this whole . . . "morality" thing. You know.

BEN I mean . . . shit, it's obvious that it's a catastrophe, right? That's . . . Why even mention that? It's beyond. I can't really find words that're even . . .

ABBY Of course you can.

BEN No, I can't! They all sound . . . lame. / No. It's impossible.

ABBY *comes out into the living area now, provoking* BEN. *He stirs.*

ABBY Try. / Okay, no words, then. Action. That's what I'm say-ing. Do you feel "not good" enough—your words, not mine—

to go out and take some action, back this feeling up with a little . . . I dunno . . . some kind of . . .

BEN You want me to, what, go down on the street . . . ?

ABBY Only if you feel like it.

BEN Of course I do. Of course, Abby . . . *but* . . . I can't.

ABBY Thank you! I *knew* it was coming.

BEN You know I can't. / You already know that!

ABBY Yeah, yeah, I know. / I just wanted to hear that you wished you could.

BEN I do. Óbviously I do.

ABBY I don't believe you.

BEN Well . . . whatever. That's not my problem.

ABBY Yeah. *(Beat.)* On my way back down here, from the store, I followed someone. I mean, I saw this woman wandering along, putting up Xeroxes of this guy. A young man. Probably not her husband, looked too young for her, but then, hey . . . *(Points to herself and* BEN.*)* I don't think so, though. But she's just shuffling along in the dark with *sunglasses* on and this stack of pages, some masking tape, doing it at random. Light poles, the sides of buildings, even on a car or two. Seriously. Didn't put the thing under the wiper but taped it right to the window. A picture of this smiling young man. In a tuxedo. "Have You Seen Him?" and a phone number. *(Beat.)* I must've trailed her for, like, ten blocks or so before I realized I'd missed my street.

BEN Wow. / Huh . . .

ABBY Yeah, "wow." / This whole city's covered in copies . . .

BEN Uh-huh. They said that on the news.

ABBY Somebody at Kinko's corporate is probably laughing his ass off right now.

BEN Yep. *(A thin smile.)* . . . So, did you help her?

ABBY What?

BEN I'm saying, did you help her out at all? Taping the signs up or anything?

ABBY No, I didn't. / I had the . . . groceries and everything . . . but umm . . . / I was just trying to . . .

BEN Oh, okay . . . / . . . ahh, "but." / . . . I see.

ABBY I get where you're going . . . / I get it, Ben.

BEN Fine. / Good. *(Beat.)* Look, it's sad, Abby, we already know that. It is. But my standing around and giving out *Twix bars* or shit like that is not gonna mean a damn thing . . . it isn't.

ABBY I *know.* It'd just be nice if you were that kind of guy . . .

BEN Well, sorry.

ABBY . . . that's all.

BEN You know why I can't, anyway. / We've discussed it.

ABBY Yeah, I know. / I *know* . . .

BEN Why I'm not answering the phone, or . . . I mean, come on.

ABBY The "meal ticket," I know.

BEN So all right, then. *(Beat.)* Doesn't mean I'm not torn up about this, that it doesn't, you know, cover my soul.

ABBY "Cover my soul"? Jesus, Ben, please . . .

BEN It "moves" me, of course it does! But we've gotta look at the implications here. What it means to *us,* our future. I don't wanna sound crass here or unfeeling or . . .

ABBY No, that could *never* happen.

BEN Listen to me! I don't . . . but do you honestly think we're not gonna rebound from this? And I don't just mean you and me, I'm saying the country as a whole. Of course we will. We'll do what it takes, go after whomever we need to, call out the *tanks* and shit, but we're gonna have the World Series, and Christmas, and all the other crap that you can count on in life. We do it, every year, no matter what's happened or is going on, we still go to the movies and buy gifts and take a two-week vacation, because that's-the-way-it-is. *(Beat.)* I'm not making light of anything, either, when I say that, or making excuses for what we've decided . . . you know . . . this is not about that. I'm saying the American way is to overcome, to conquer, to come out on top. And we do it by spending and eating and screwing our women harder than anyone else. That's all I'm saying.

ABBY That's really moving . . . / It's like seeing a Norman Rockwell for the first time.

BEN It is, though! That's what we do. It's what we're good at . . . / Come on, gimme a break . . .

ABBY It's just . . . I mean, it's sooo, what, *outlandish*, you saying that! I don't even know where to . . .

BEN I'm not saying it's "great," I'm saying it's a fact! This is a national disaster, yes . . . *until* the next time the Yankees win the pennant, then we'll all move on from there. Sorry, but it's true. *(Beat.)* And I do understand the "big picture" here. The larger context, I mean. I do.

ABBY Yeah? You've been keeping track on CNN, or . . .

BEN No.

ABBY . . . somebody send by an interoffice memo?

BEN No, not exactly. I just . . . sort of . . . *know.* You know?

ABBY You "know." Oh. *(Beat.)* You mean, like Kreskin or something? Like that?

BEN . . . You're being facetious now, right? / You didn't win the argument, so now you're gonna . . .

ABBY Very good. / See . . . you're not that much in shock, are you?

BEN Guess not. *(Beat.)* Actually, I don't know who Kreskin is, I just figured you were being mean-spirited and went with it.

ABBY Touché. *(Beat.)* You don't remember who the Amazing Kreskin was? Seriously?

BEN No.

ABBY Come on!

BEN I don't . . . I'm sure it's one of those "you wouldn't understand" things. I probably wasn't old enough . . .

ABBY Well, at least you're still sweet.

BEN I don't mean that you're . . . I'm just saying . . . whatever.

ABBY Yep, that's us. "Whatever." Pretty much sums it up. *(Beat.)* Kreskin was a mystic. Well, not a mystic, really, not that, but just this guy on TV who would—looked a little like Austin Powers, in a way—he was a psychic, I guess that's what you'd call him. Psychic. He'd walk around the studio, he had this show on television, Sundays, and he'd wander through the place telling people stuff about their lives. Reading their minds. Calling out the name of their dead dog, their mother's birth date, crap like that. Figuring out where they lost their keys or their way in life, that kind of thing. Even card tricks. Sort of. That's who Kreskin was . . . around the time of *Wild Kingdom* and *Disney* and all those shows. Every Sunday night. When I was a teenager. *(Beat.)* Just forget it.

BEN No, but, I mean . . . what was the point of that?

ABBY I don't know. I really don't.

BEN Oh. Okay.

ABBY Yeah. Let's stop right there . . . at those frightening generational gaps that rage between us.

BEN You're not that much older, Abby, really. I mean, a bit.

ABBY Ben . . .

BEN Well, a dozen years, but . . .

ABBY Just leave it. *(BEN nods and stops there. The cell phone begins to ring again. They look at each other as he switches it off.)* Audie Murphy would be so proud.

BEN Who's that?

ABBY No one. *(She chuckles.)* Don't worry about it.

BEN Another member of the ol' Sunday-night lineup or something?

ABBY You're such a shit.

BEN Yeah, and don't forget I'm in shock. Imagine what I can do when I'm really firing on all cylinders.

ABBY Oh, I'm well aware, believe me. Believe you me . . .

BEN No, come on, go ahead . . . who is this Murphy person?

ABBY Geez, you're just, like, a complete cultural moron.

BEN Yep. Pretty much, yeah, and you know why?

ABBY Yes . . . because it doesn't get you anything. There's no *reward* for knowing any of it. Trivia. / It's frivolous to you.

BEN Exactly! / That's *exactly* my point.

ABBY You ever hear that "knowledge is its own reward"?

BEN Knowledge is shit, okay? "Knowledge for Knowledge's Sake" is pure *bull*shit. *(Beat.)* All learning ever does is remind you of what you haven't got. Teaches you about new stuff you'll never be or have. Because unless you can apply that knowledge and *do* something with it, it's useless. It's crap. Worthless shit. An MBA is one thing, but *Jeopardy!* is for assholes . . .

ABBY Well, well . . . Goliath awakes.

BEN I'm just saying . . .

ABBY I heard you.

BEN I'm just saying it, that's all.

ABBY And it's been noted. *(Beat.)* Duly noted.

BEN Don't.

ABBY What?

BEN You know what. Just don't, okay?

ABBY I don't know what you're talking about.

BEN Yes, you do. Of course you do. I've told you not to . . .

ABBY And don't say "just don't" to me, Ben.

BEN I'm saying "don't say that," that's what I'm saying. You know what I'm saying, we've had this argument a hundred times since we've been . . . / Yes, we have, we're always . . .

ABBY No, we haven't. / We never *get* to the argument because any time you've ever told me "just don't," I tell you to NEVER say that to me!

BEN Yeah, well, just don't . . . I mean it.

ABBY Oooooooh. You're so sexy when you're being a prick.

BEN Abby, just . . . don't.

ABBY Stop it! / Don't say that!!

BEN You stop! / I said "don't" first!!

ABBY STOP THAT!!

BEN You!!

ABBY What did I say?! *What?*

BEN You know what you said, what you always say!

ABBY What?!!

BEN "It's been noted! Duly noted!!" You know you said that, you say it all the time.

ABBY Oh. *(Beat.)* I said that again?

BEN Yes, you did.

ABBY I didn't even realize it, I'm sorry.

BEN Fine, then.

ABBY Fine.

BEN I just don't want that. / I won't take it. Seriously.

ABBY What? / What, Ben . . . what won't you "take"?

BEN You know. / *That.* Being treated like one of your . . . under-lings.

ABBY No. / . . . You are, though, Ben.

BEN I am not! And I won't be treated like it.

ABBY Well, I'm not trying to start something, I'm not . . . I prom-ise, but . . .

BEN I don't work under you.

ABBY No?

BEN No, I do not. I hold a position that supports yours.

ABBY Yes, you do.

BEN . . . is subordinate to yours, maybe.

ABBY True.

BEN I get paid less.

ABBY Quite a bit less.

BEN *Somewhat* less. Right. That's all true . . .

ABBY But . . . ?

BEN *But* I'm not "under" you. You do not tower over me in some literal or figurative way.

ABBY This may be drifting toward semantics . . .

BEN No, it's not. I have a point and it's not. *(Beat.)* I am your colleague. Your co-worker. Your partner.

ABBY Okay, Ben, I get it.

BEN No, I just want to point out that . . .

ABBY Geez, I wish you were this specific when you tell me to do that one thing with my tongue that you like . . .

BEN That's not funny.

ABBY Yeah, it is.

BEN No, it isn't. At all.

ABBY It's pretty funny.

BEN No, it's not. It's not at all funny . . . not when I'm trying to say something. Something about us.

ABBY You've said it, Ben. I-get-it. I do. And I'm sorry if what I say sometimes hurts you.

BEN Well, it does. Sometimes. When you do.

ABBY Was that a sentence?

BEN I'm serious!

ABBY Fine.

BEN You belittle me. You make me feel small.

ABBY And yet, somehow, I don't tower over you . . .

BEN Abby, stop it!!

ABBY Okay, okay. I was kidding. Please.

BEN Whatever.

ABBY I was. Fair enough? Can we stop?

BEN Yes. *(Beat.)* And I'm sorry I said the other thing. The "just don't" thing.

ABBY All right.

BEN I wasn't saying it at you, anyway, I was . . .

ABBY I know, but . . .

BEN I just meant don't say the "duly noted" thing, like I'm some . . . *Egyptian slave,* or whatever. / Anyway . . .

ABBY I accept your apology. / Yes, anyway . . .

BEN Okay. *(Beat.)* And if I am "under" you, I mean, if people would say that about me, behind my back, some Old World phrase like that . . . it's because you have never, in your infinite wisdom, seen fit to *promote* me. *(A pause in which BEN suddenly stands and dusts himself off a bit. Moves the pillows around. Sits back down and ponders his cell phone. ABBY watches.)* Who the hell is Audrey Murphy, anyway?

ABBY It's "Audie." He's a guy.

BEN Oh. Audie is a guy's name?

ABBY Yes. And anyway, it's no big thing.

BEN No, come on, you said it, you might as well . . .

ABBY It was just a . . .

BEN He must be somebody important. Somebody who does something better than me or you wouldn't have brought him up.

ABBY Ben, honestly, it's not a big deal.

BEN I wanna know! I do.

ABBY Oh, for God's . . . *(Beat.)* Did you ever see *To Hell and Back*?

BEN Uh-uh. What is that, on the TV?

ABBY No. It's a movie. Well, he wrote the book first, and then . . .

BEN So he's an author. Big deal.

ABBY He acted in it as well. The movie.

BEN He did?

ABBY Yes.

BEN Oh. Now he's an actor, too.

ABBY Uh-huh.

BEN Did he play himself?

ABBY Umm . . . yes, he did. I guess so, but . . .

BEN Well, that's not really acting, then, is it?

ABBY He was . . . Yes, of course it is! It's still acting.

BEN No, it's not . . . not technically.

ABBY Ben, yes, it is . . . He was re-creating what happened to him during the war. World War II. But I'm sure they did many takes of each scene, over and over, like they do. Re-enacting it. So I'd call that acting, wouldn't you?

BEN I guess. Playing himself, though. That's kinda weak.

ABBY He was very good. And he did that other movie . . . called, ahh, you know, the . . . / Red Badge of Courage.

BEN No . . . / The Civil War one?

ABBY Yes! See, you're not an absolute moron.

BEN No, even I was forced to take a lit class or two. (Beat.) That was Stephen Crane. He died young, / twenty-nine or something.

ABBY Well, he played the lead part in that as well . . . / Huh.

BEN Another war part. It's the same thing.

ABBY What do you mean?

BEN I'm saying the guy was no Brando, that's what I'm saying. And yes, I know who Brando is. *(Beat.)* He did a couple war pictures . . . What is the *point* here?

ABBY No point. Sorry I brought it up.

BEN No, uh-uh, I turned off my phone. I didn't answer it and turned it off and you said your "Andy Murphy" crack, so tell me why he's so . . .

ABBY "Audie." His name was "Audie Murphy." Jesus . . .

BEN Why'd you say that to me?

ABBY I was being ironic.

BEN Oh God . . . no, not that, please.

ABBY I was.

BEN Not Abby Prescott's famous fallback position . . . Irony!

ABBY I was and I'm sorry.

BEN And so . . . just where was the irony? Huh?

ABBY Ben, I don't want to get into . . . *(Beat.)* Look at the news.

BEN Fuck the news! I don't give a shit about the news!! *(He reaches down and scoops up the remote, savagely pushing the off button.)* I want to know what the hell is so *ironic* about some Audie Murphy in reference to me!!

ABBY *looks squarely at* BEN *and then picks up some cheese. Pops it in her mouth. Finishes it.*

ABBY He was a hero.

BEN A what?

ABBY Ha! *(She laughs.)* You don't even recognize the word.

BEN What do you mean, "hero"? What kind of hero?

ABBY A war hero. A hero in the World War. That's what he was, and that's why I said it.

BEN Oh. *(Beat.)* A hero, huh?

ABBY Apparently so. Medal of Honor and all that.

BEN And so . . . the irony is . . .

ABBY When juxtaposed with you . . .

BEN Got it. I get it. "Duly noted." (ABBY *glances sharply over at* BEN, *which makes him smile.*) Ha-ha-ha. How ironic. How utter fuckingly ironic.

ABBY Just forget it.

BEN Wow, that was a good one! / Jesus, you oughta be on *Leno*.

ABBY Ben . . . / Knock it off.

BEN No, I'm serious, you should've ended up in that one lesbian chick's video thing, you're so goddamn clever.

ABBY Who?

BEN That one long-haired chick, hates guys. The lesbian one. / You know, you've got the CD!

ABBY I don't know who you're . . . / No . . .

BEN With the name . . . / The big-time name . . . from Canada.

ABBY Who? / . . . Alanis Morissette?

BEN That's her! You should've been in that car with her and her four other *selves*, driving around, you're so wonderfully ironic. *(Beat.)* Bitch, call me "ironic."

ABBY She's not a lesbian. / I'm just telling you . . .

BEN So what? / What do I care?

ABBY I know you don't care. Because it's trivia.

BEN No, trivial, that's what it is. *Trivial*. And she looks like one, anyway, so that's enough.

ABBY God, you frighten me sometimes. You really do.

BEN I don't exactly sleep like a baby next to you, either, honey.

ABBY No, I mean it. You do. *(Beat.)* And how the hell did you remember she's *Canadian* if you don't like trivia?

BEN Because VH1, as usual, played the shit out of it when it first came out.

ABBY Yeah, but why would you . . . ?

BEN I watch VH1.

ABBY What? When do you ever sit down and watch . . . ?

BEN I do, and it was always on . . . with the pop-up things . . .

ABBY Yes, but that's still pretty . . .

BEN My daughter liked it! There, how's that? How's that for a reality check, huh? Because *my* daughter liked the song . . .

ABBY Okay.

BEN Because my twelve-year-old, who is probably sobbing her eyes out right now, wondering where her *daddy* is, likes the same fucking song that you just used to tease me with! That's how I know!! *(Beat.)* Better?

ABBY All right, Ben, I'm sorry. / I am . . .

BEN Great, you're sorry. / That's really terrific. *(Beat.)* Yep.

ABBY Don't.

BEN What?

ABBY Stop it.

BEN Stop what?

ABBY Just *stop* it . . . Don't make this about you.

BEN What do you mean?

ABBY I'm saying, don't make this thing that's happened, this whole . . . unbelievable thing that is going on out there right now . . . just about you. Because it's not. It isn't.

BEN Oh, it's not, huh?

ABBY No. It-is-not.

BEN . . . (*He is about to say something else, but thinks better of it, bites his tongue. He crosses over to one of the windows and looks out.*) Jesus.

ABBY Indeed.

BEN I mean . . .

ABBY I was just out there, remember?

BEN Yes.

ABBY Getting you your cheese. I went out there to . . .

BEN I know you did.

ABBY You know how *hard* it is to find Havarti at four in the morning? / The shelves are empty. People are snapping up shit like it was . . .

BEN No, but . . . / I'm sure they are.

ABBY Well, they are. Since yesterday. *(Beat.)* Do you want some?

BEN No, it's okay. Thank you, though. *(He moves to another window.)* Look at the . . . un-fucking-believable.

ABBY Uh-huh.

BEN You know? I mean, I know that's inadequate, but . . . shit. Look at it out there! It's . . . I mean, those buildings are just, like, gone.

ABBY Yes. *(Beat.)* The cheese is very good. You should eat something.

BEN No thanks.

ABBY All right. I'll put it in the fridge. Put it away.

BEN Okay.

ABBY For later.

BEN Uh-huh. *(Beat.)* How many?

ABBY What?

BEN People missing. Do they . . . ?

ABBY I thought you were following the . . .

BEN I am, but . . . / CNN keeps upping the . . . tally thing.

ABBY Thousands, I guess. / Something like that.

BEN Dead, or missing?

ABBY Same thing. I mean . . . looks like, anyway.

BEN I suppose.

ABBY They're saying close to five. Around there.

BEN God.

ABBY All those people . . . just . . . *(She snaps her fingers.)*

BEN Yeah.

ABBY Including you.

BEN Mmm-hmm.

ABBY You've been lost, Ben. Just like that. Up in smoke.
(BEN *nods thoughtfully at this, moves to yet another window. Tries to look down the street.* ABBY *steps out toward him.*) I wouldn't do that too much. People do know you around here. Well, they don't "know" you, but . . . you know.

BEN Right. That's true.

ABBY I mean, I'm not sure anyone could ever really *know* Ben Harcourt, but you see what I'm saying.

BEN Uh-huh. I get it.

ABBY They know the face. That wonderful face of yours . . . / At the mailbox. Coming up the stairs. You are "known."

BEN Great. / Well, I'll be careful, then.

BEN *steps away, wandering the room a bit. Stops in front of the*
TV and turns it on.

ABBY Good. I mean, you wouldn't wanna blow your cover just
   yet, right, sweetie?

BEN You know, Abby, that's . . .

ABBY I just calls 'em like I sees 'em.

BEN *just waves her off, too tired of this to engage anymore.* ABBY
watches. Suddenly, ABBY*'s home phone rings three times.* BEN
and ABBY *stare at each other. It stops ringing.*

BEN Looks like it might be higher. / Maybe six . . .

ABBY Huh. / That's horrible.

BEN Shit . . . six thousand people. Fuck.

ABBY Unless they're all hiding out at their girlfriends' houses.

BEN Jesus, that's cynical.

ABBY I thought that was one of the rules of disaster . . . to keep
   it light.

BEN Not *that* light.

ABBY Sorry.

BEN Forget it. *(Beat.)* It's like February. You know? If I just
   woke up, from maybe a long sleep or something, and went to
   the window, I'd think it was the middle of winter.

ABBY Well, it doesn't feel like winter. Not out there. / Not at all.

BEN I didn't say that . . . / I'm saying what it looks like, okay?
   It's not a definitive weather forecast, for chrissakes. I'm just
   saying how it *looks* . . . / Like the last place on Earth.

ABBY Oh. / If it was snow, we could go down and enjoy it.

BEN Mmm-hmm.

ABBY Make angels and go skiing, and all that shit we used to do.

BEN Yep.

ABBY Except you can't go outside, right? Don't wanna be *spotted*.

BEN Why do you have to keep saying . . . ?

ABBY Just pointing out the "irony." Sorry.

BEN Whatever.

ABBY But if it was, snow, I mean, and none of this . . . stuff . . . had ever happened, then we could. We could go play.

BEN Yeah.

ABBY Like when we first met.

BEN Sure.

ABBY Remember?

BEN 'Course. Vermont . . .

ABBY Yeah . . . You sliced your hand open on the binding. *(She smiles.)* The edge of your ski binding.

BEN Right! Had to get a stitch or two, didn't I?

ABBY Exactly. Three, I think . . .

BEN Stupid thing . . . the corner was all exposed. *(Beat.)* Still, it was a great trip.

ABBY Yep. Back when we liked each other.

BEN *looks over at* ABBY, *uncertain.* ABBY *glances at him, but returns to putting away the cheese and the rest of the groceries.*

BEN What's that supposed to mean?

ABBY Nothing.

BEN No, seriously.

ABBY Nothing, Ben. Not anything.

BEN I still like you . . . What do you mean?

ABBY I'm saying those first days were lovely. Really special. That's all I'm saying.

BEN I do, too! I mean, feel that way. *(Beat.)* Listen, God, Abby, you gotta know, I mean, I know that you *know* . . . This is not me. Like me, that is. This whole thing. Idea. I'm not normally like that. I just . . . But when I looked at it, for even a second, all I could see is, yeah, it's sad, it's just unbelievably *horrid* and all that shit, but . . . this is it. This is the moment. *Our* moment. Everything comes down to what we decide right here. Today. I use my Discover card or get picked up on a *mini-mart* video camera, it's over. Finished. The whole thing's lost. And so that's why I'm . . . you know . . . Fuck. I dunno.

ABBY Then good. *(Beat.)* I just wish, whatever happens, it could always be like that. Like Vermont.

BEN It can. Abby, that's what all this . . . *(Beat.)* Christ, that's what this is about! It can be like that now. Always. That's why we're . . . doing it.

ABBY I guess so . . .

BEN Right? I mean, Jesus . . . you think I was born this way, like some cutthroat *pirate* of the high seas? Huh? Hell, I'm just trying to muddle through, that's all, just muddle my fucking way through to middle age, see if I can make it that far. You like trivia so goddamn much, well, here's a little tidbit for ya . . . I'm *faking* it. Okay? Totally getting by on fumes. I put my *game* face on and go out there and I'm scared shitless. *(Beat.)* You know what? I take that back . . . This *is* me. I've screwed up every step of my life, Abby, I'm not afraid to admit it. Happy to, actually, I am happy to sing it out there for anybody who wants to hear. I always take the easy route, do it faster, simpler, you know, whatever it takes to get it done, be liked, get by. That's me. Cheated in school, screwed over my friends, took whatever I could get from whomever I could take it from. My marriage, there's a goddamn fiasco, of which you're intimately aware. The kids . . . I barely register as a dad, I'm sure, but compared to the other shit in my life, I'm Doctor-fucking-*Spock*. No matter what I do or have done, they adore the hell out of me, and I'm totally knocked out by that. What kids are like. Yeah. *(Beat.)* And you, let's not forget you. *Us.* Okay, yes, I haven't done all that I've promised, said I'd do, I fuck up along the way. All right. But I'm trying, this time out—with you, I mean—I have been trying. Don't know what it looks like, feels to you, but I have made a real go of us, and that is not a lie. It isn't. And so then, yesterday . . . through all the smoke and fear and just, I dunno, *apocalyptic* shit . . . I see a way for us to go for it, to totally erase the past—and I don't think it makes me Lucifer or a criminal or some bad man because I noticed it. I really don't. We've been given something here. A chance to . . . I don't know what, to wash away a lot of the, just, rotten crap we've done. More than anything else, that's what this is. A chance. I know it is.

ABBY Yeah, but it's tainted . . . / . . . it's a fluke.

BEN What? / No, it's not that, no, it's . . .

ABBY We got lucky. Or, more specifically . . . *you* did. But you didn't earn it.

BEN What're you talking about?

ABBY I'm just saying that it was a happy coincidence that you managed to be over here at my place yesterday morning, getting your proverbial cock sucked, when it happened . . . that's all. *(Beat.)* Right?

BEN I guess. Yes.

ABBY The one day out of the year you're supposed to be down there for us and you decide to skip out, come over, get some head . . . that's not bad.

BEN So?

ABBY So . . . there's probably a lot of spouses out there right now who wish their dearly departed would've stopped to pick up a nice Frappuccino or dropped off that roll of film they were carrying around in their pocket . . . hell, maybe paid for a *blow job*, even. Whatever it takes to stay alive. *(Beat.)* I'm saying you really dodged a bullet there.

BEN Plane. I dodged a plane.

ABBY Ooooohhh. Careful with the humor thing, remember?

BEN Yeah . . . *(Beat.)* That's a shitty thing to say.

ABBY Even if it's true?

BEN Yes. Even then.

ABBY Sorry. I'm an honest person . . . *(She laughs.)* Mostly.

BEN Yeah, make sure you slip that one in. "Mostly."

ABBY I believe you just may be pointing a finger at me, Mr. Harcourt.

BEN I just may be, Ms. Prescott.

ABBY Ahh. And what, in your mind, have I been dishonest about?

BEN Nothing . . . I mean, other than, oh . . . your entire life. *(He sits back down on this, pulls out the cell phone again. He turns it on and sets it on one knee.)*

ABBY I'm being dishonest?

BEN Just a little.

ABBY About what?

BEN Come on . . .

ABBY No, seriously, what're you . . . ?

BEN Which category . . . work, rest, or play?

ABBY You tell me.

BEN Well, umm . . . me. There's that topic.

ABBY You?

BEN Yes. I think so, yes. / For three years . . .

ABBY How? / What, that we're an *item*?

BEN Yeah. That.

ABBY Oh, come on.

BEN What?

ABBY People know that. Jesus, I mean . . . *lots* of people! Well, not your wife, maybe, but that's about it.

BEN That's not true.

ABBY She knows?

BEN No, Jesus . . . I mean people. People don't know.

ABBY Ben, come on. I'm sure they do.

BEN I'm serious. We've been cautious.

ABBY We have? / When?

BEN Yes! / What're you *talking* about? I'm always careful to . . .

ABBY What, call on your cell phone? / Keep my keys hidden in the ficus tree at the office?

BEN Yeah. / And other stuff.

ABBY Shit, Ben, *please* . . .

BEN I'm not kidding!

ABBY Neither am I!

BEN Hey, I've never told anybody about us. No one. Ever.

ABBY I know that.

BEN I've been a steel trap this whole time.

ABBY Of course you have.

BEN I have!

ABBY I know, Ben. I'm *agreeing* with you.

BEN So then, what?

ABBY I have been.

BEN What?

ABBY Indiscreet.

BEN You have . . . what? Told someone?

ABBY Yes.

BEN Shit. I mean . . . why the fuck would you do that? Huh?

ABBY Because I used to be proud of the fact.

BEN Oh.

ABBY Back whenever. Don't worry, I'm not a complete kamikaze . . . It was family, not at the office.

BEN I didn't mean . . . you know . . .

ABBY Anyway, it was a long time ago. *Years* ago. I'm sure people've forgotten . . . / I know / have.

BEN I wasn't being . . . / Come on, you know what I'm saying.

ABBY Of course I do. I've always known.

BEN Okay, then.

ABBY You like fucking the boss, but you don't want it getting around.

BEN Abby . . .

ABBY Get it. I got it. *(Beat.)* But maybe you should ask the boss sometime if she likes fucking you.

BEN *looks over at this.* ABBY *wanders to the window and looks out. Comes slowly back into the room as* BEN *follows her with his eyes. After a moment,* ABBY*'s phone rings, then stops after three rings. Silence as they look at each other.*

BEN And what's that supposed to mean?

ABBY Just a suggestion.

BEN Ask you if . . . what?

ABBY How I feel about the two of us.

BEN I know how you feel about us.

ABBY You do?

BEN Of course, I . . . yes, sure. I do.

ABBY Oh.

BEN Don't I?

ABBY Sure you do.

BEN I mean . . .

ABBY I'm sure you *think* you do, anyway.

BEN All right, this is . . . I know what you're doing.

ABBY What?

BEN I see what . . . I know this trick.

ABBY I'm not tricking you.

BEN Yes, uh-huh, yes, you are. This is the "make Ben feel insecure" thing. / I know this game.

ABBY Don't be insecure. / It's not a game . . .

BEN Listen, you don't like having sex with me, you wouldn't have it. It's that simple. / You're that kind of woman.

ABBY Nothing's that simple . . . / You think so?

BEN I *know* so. (*Beat.*) You don't like some assistant at work, they're outta there in twenty minutes. You don't fancy a *salt shaker* in the cafeteria, it's changed. If you didn't want us coming over here, or sneaking off at conferences and me banging the shit outta you, we wouldn't be doing it.

ABBY Really?

BEN Yeah, really. I mean, you're the fucking "guy" in this relationship, let's not kid ourselves . . .

ABBY Okay, Ben . . .

BEN Ms. Prescott sports the Haggar slacks around here.

ABBY Well, *somebody's* got to!

BEN Yeah, but somebody doesn't have to be an overdominating cunt about it . . . *(Beat.)* Sorry, shit, I didn't mean . . . you know . . .

ABBY Oh, I'm sure you meant that in the best possible way.

BEN No, I just . . .

ABBY As you always say, Ben . . . whatever.

ABBY *heads back to the safety of the kitchen.* BEN *looks at the phone and shakes it, listens.*

BEN I don't have any sexual problems.

ABBY I wasn't saying you did. Or implying it.

BEN Fine.

ABBY But somehow, as usual, you were able to turn something about me into a thing about you.

BEN What? When . . . ?

ABBY I said you should ask me if I like doing it with you. Not that you had a problem . . . per se.

BEN Why wouldn't you like doing it with me?

ABBY That's not what I . . .

BEN We're great together, why wouldn't you . . . ? I do not get you! What the hell are we even . . .

ABBY Don't worry, Ben, I like *screwing* you just fine.

BEN Oh.

ABBY See, no worries . . .

BEN I didn't think so. That there was a problem, I mean.

ABBY I didn't say there wasn't a problem.

BEN Well . . . then, I . . . What don't you like?

ABBY The rest.

BEN What "rest"? There is no other. *(Beat.)* You mean, like, oral?

ABBY No! God, you're like a twelve-year-old.

BEN Well, I'm missing something.

ABBY I know. Me too.

BEN No, I mean, you're just going in loops here, and I'm . . .

ABBY Ben, come on, you're a goddamn grown-up! Stop it. *(Beat.)* I don't like what we've been doing.

BEN Oh. You mean the, you know, secrecy and all that. The not telling people about us.

ABBY No, not even that. I mean, I don't *love* it, not at all, but I'm whatever about it . . . I'm talking about the rest. Other stuff.

BEN Abby, *what*? Shit, I don't . . .

ABBY Ben, God, you can be thick. It's sexual harassment, you know that.

BEN . . . No, it's not.

ABBY Yes, it is. Yes. Very much so.

BEN That's not, no, it's consensual, what we've got, it's . . .

ABBY Doesn't matter, Ben, it doesn't. How many times have you gone to those seminars and shit?! I mean . . . a million.

BEN I don't *listen* at those things, do you?

ABBY As a matter of fact, yeah, I do. I'm usually the one *giving* them, remember?

BEN That's true.

ABBY And when I'm standing up there, going on about an "empowered workspace," and all the while I'm fucking one of my employees, how do you think I feel? Huh?

BEN I don't know . . . clever?

ABBY No, Ben, not clever . . . I feel like shit. Like a fucking Judas, and just plain awful. All right? That's how. *(Beat.)* You don't think I've fretted over promoting you, or not promoting you, or whatever the hell I see fit . . . ? *(Beat.)* Every second of every day since we've been together I've worried about this. Us. Worried myself sick if we're talking in the hall too long or we kiss at a restaurant or I lean over and grab your knee under some conference table in *San Diego*—I may like it, usually feels great while we're doing it, but something inside me, up inside me somewhere, is screaming, "You fucking idiot! You stupid needy bitch . . ." After everything I've worked for, the *pounds* of shit I've eaten to get where I am . . . to blow it all on a piece of ass.

BEN I'm a piece of ass?

ABBY Sometimes, yeah, Ben . . . you are.

BEN Oh.

ABBY I'm sorry, but . . .

BEN No, I mean, that's how you think of this?

ABBY On occasion. *(Beat.)* At first, maybe, yes, I did.

BEN *thinks about this a moment, considering the thought. He nods.*

BEN Well, I'm fine with that.

ABBY You are?

BEN Absolutely. Not that I only think of you in that way, but a lot of the time, yeah . . . you're basically a nice lay. True, a lay that I respect and work for and enjoy taking out for a *Coney dog* & fries . . .

ABBY Charming . . .

BEN It's true. I mean, I like being with you, want to spend our lives together, but sure, I've said that to myself a number of times: "She may be the boss, but ol' Abby's simply one hell of a sweet fuck."

ABBY See?

BEN What?

ABBY . . . You just did the same thing.

BEN What thing? / . . . no . . .

ABBY The "boss" thing. You relate to us in terms of who we are at work, our positions . . . / You just did!

BEN "Listen, sister, the only position I relate to you in is when you're facedown on this rug, faux or not . . ." / No . . . I'm playing!

ABBY Oh really? / You sure it's not a control issue?

BEN Yes! *(Beat.)* I don't care if you're my project director or a waitress at the corner deli . . . I like you for you.

ABBY Then why do we always do it from behind?

BEN We don't.

ABBY *Always.* From the first day since. All fours, facedown, never looking me in the eye.

BEN I'm . . . That's not fair. No.

Neil LaBute

ABBY You go down on me occasionally, that's true . . . because you think you're good at it. / You're not, by the way, for the record. Good. You're okay, not terrible, but by no means outstanding.

BEN No, I enjoy . . . / Wow, let 'er rip while we're . . .

ABBY And you'll let me give you head. Which I'm free to do any which way I like . . . standing, sitting, on a train, in a plane . . .

BEN We've never . . .

ABBY On a boat, with a goat . . . It's like I'm fucking *Dr. Seuss*!

BEN Abby . . . this is so out of whack that I can't even . . .

ABBY But you never even *glance* at me, Ben, when we're making love. Not ever. *(Beat.)* Why is that?

BEN So, is this something . . . what, you've just been lying in wait for the right . . .?

ABBY Yeah, maybe.

BEN Okay. Well . . . umm . . . let's see . . .

ABBY You don't think it's just a little bit of "I'm gonna let the ol' gal have it for getting that promotion over me"? Not just a *touch* of that?

BEN No. I don't.

ABBY Sure? I mean, you barely used to acknowledge me when you first started at our office . . . not even a smile in the morning, we're on the elevator together. / We had that whole competitive thing going right off the bat, don't say we didn't.

BEN I was new, that's no big . . . / Maybe, yeah, maybe so, but . . .

ABBY But then I get a boost, right, I snag the position we've both been gunning for, and *bang*, like, a month later, you're suddenly jockeying for private dinners out and discussions after work.

BEN You're my boss! What the hell . . .

ABBY I'm just saying, your timing, like yesterday, is impeccable.

BEN Hey, we started working together . . . I fell for you, it's not a crime.

ABBY Ahh, actually, in some states it is . . . you're married.

BEN Yeah, well . . .

ABBY And then we got together—on that retreat the first time, remember? Up in Connecticut—and that was pretty much the last moment you looked me fully in the face. Three years ago . . .

BEN This is crazy.

ABBY I know. I know it is.

BEN I want to be with you , . . together, with *you*, for the rest of my life. Now, if that's . . .

ABBY I'm not talking about that, I'm . . .

BEN If you wanna find some way to *ruin* this, that's fine. Go ahead.

ABBY *stops for a moment and studies* BEN. *Watches to see if his body betrays him at all. It doesn't.*

ABBY It just . . . makes a girl wonder.

BEN Fine. If you wanna . . . fine. Missionary it is . . . fuck. *(Beat.)* Anyway, it's probably just guilt or whatever. The "doggie-style" thing . . .

ABBY Guilt? / Not Oedipal, I hope.

BEN Yeah, you know . . . / NO! I mean about cheating and stuff
. . . Maybe it's just hard to look you in the face or, God, I
dunno.

ABBY Hell, Ben, I feel guilty. Every moment. But I still wouldn't
mind making eye contact once a week.

BEN It just hurts sometimes. That's all.

ABBY Then don't do it. It's a pretty simple equation.

BEN Abby . . .

ABBY Seriously.

BEN Why're we even . . . ?

ABBY I mean it. If you feel so "not good," then stop putting your
thing in me and go the hell away . . . / Or at least switch your
phone on and take your wife's call.

BEN That's not what I'm . . . / Awww, screw this.

ABBY Let 'em know you're alive, do that much! / Quit hiding out
in my loft and do the *right* thing, I mean, shit!!

BEN I don't want that! / I want you!!

ABBY Oh.

BEN I *want* you, Abby . . . that's what I want.

*They both come to a stop and stare at each other, having let out
far more than they expected to. Silence. The sound of sirens out
there somewhere.*

ABBY Then why don't you say that every few days, just so I'm in
on it. Okay?

BEN Yeah, sorry, I should. *(Beat.)* I do want you, though . . . I do.

ABBY I'm glad.

BEN And I don't expect anything for it or care who knows it or will *ever* use it against you . . . I just-want-you. That's all. *(Beat.)* By the way, I enjoy having sex from behind. It feels nice and, like, intimate. I love being with you like that. I do.

ABBY Thank you, Ben. That's very . . . thanks. *(Beat.)* It's funny, I probably shouldn't even go there, but—it's comical, almost . . . almost comical the things you can imagine while you're making love that way. Facedown. Turned away from a person. It is to me, anyway. The ideas, or images, or, you know, just *stuff* . . . that goes through your head if you do it that way for too long. Ha! Wow, it's . . . I don't know. Just funny.

BEN What do you mean? Like . . . like what?

ABBY Oh, just things. Things that you'd never expect, or be pre-pared for, or anything; visions that will just suddenly appear as you're kneeling there. Doing it. Having it done *to* you. 'Cause that's what it's like when you have sex that way all the time, like it's being done to you. That it really doesn't matter to the person back there who "it" is. Just that it— meaning, a backside—is there and available and willing. And so a lot of the time when you're going at it, my mind has just drifted off and I'll think such crazy thoughts . . . sometimes fantasies, like it's somebody else, a lover I've taken, or that I'm being attacked, jumped in an alleyway by some person . . . or I'll just make lists, "to do" lists for work or shopping or whatnot. I can remember figuring out all my Christmas ideas one night in Orlando at the Hyatt there, during one of our lit-tle . . . on the carpet, as I recall . . . do you remember that night? We had those adjoining suites . . . that was a nice conference. In fact, that might've been where I first noticed your particular bent for . . . well, you know. My *back porch.*

BEN Abby . . . why don't we just . . .

ABBY But most of the time I just imagine that it's your wife. Lately that's the thought that I can't seem to get out of my head. That it's your sweet little Mrs. from the suburbs behind me with one of those, umm, things—those, like, *strappy* things that you buy at sex shops—and she's just going to town on me. Banging away for hours because of what I've done to her life, and you know what? I let her. I let her do it, because somewhere inside I feel like I probably deserve it, it's true . . . and when I think about it, when I stop and really take it in for a moment, it doesn't actually feel that much different than when we do it. Honestly. I mean, in some ways, who better? She knows what you do it like, the speed, rhythm, all that. Unless you do it with her all pretty and tender and who knows what. Do you? No, probably not . . . she's probably read the ol' *mattress tag* more times than even me, God bless 'er. *(Beat.)* I dunno. Maybe that's what Hell is, in the end. All of your wrongful shit played out there in front of you while you're being pumped from behind by someone you've hurt. That you've screwed over in life. Or worse, worse still . . . some person who doesn't really love you anymore. No one to ever look at again, make contact with. Just you being fucked as your life splashes out across this big headboard in the Devil's bedroom. Maybe. Even if that's not it, even if Hell is all fire and sulfur and that sort of thing, it couldn't be much worse than that.

BEN No, I s'ppose not.

Sirens in the distance. ABBY *goes to a window.*

ABBY So . . . what do you think they'll say about you?

BEN Huh?

ABBY You know, at the wake or . . . whatever it is that your people do. I mean, between the potato salad and cold meats,
what kind of speeches do you think your loved ones're gonna
make?

BEN About me?

ABBY Yes.

BEN I dunno.

ABBY Oh come on . . .

BEN Seriously, no, I don't wanna do that.

ABBY We're just imagining . . .

BEN Yeah, but it's creepy. That is spooky shit, and I don't wanna
think about it . . .

ABBY What do you care, you're *dead.* *(She smiles.)* I bet they
get you a nice big stone. With the metal plaque and whatnot.
You said your wife's good at that kind of thing.

BEN No, I didn't.

ABBY Yes, you said . . . / . . . still . . .

BEN I said decorating. / Matching up *towels* and wallpaper and
shit, not funerals.

ABBY Same idea, just . . . permanent.

BEN Whatever.

ABBY Hell, maybe the company'll pay for it. Least they can do.

BEN Right.

ABBY After losing one so young and gifted . . .

BEN Okay, okay . . .

ABBY Probably get you one of those kinds with an angel perched up on it . . . maybe a little flame thing, even. That'd be cute . . . It's probably a tax write-off, too.

BEN You know, Abby, you're . . .

ABBY What'll it say?—hmm?—your little marker—do you think?

BEN What do you mean?

ABBY Your epitaph. I mean, if you could write it. I'm sure it'll have the "loving husband, father, brother" bullshit, no doubt; but if it was you out there with the chisel, what would you put?·

BEN *starts to say something, then stops. Considers. Then:*

BEN "He was okay." / Yeah . . .

ABBY "*Okay*"? / Why on earth would you . . . ?

BEN Because "okay" is not such a bad thing. It's pretty fucking underrated, actually.

ABBY Your big chance to sound good and you go with "okay." Wow.

BEN Let me tell you something, there's a shitload of people out there, right now, who would like to be just "okay." Would *love* it. It's . . . I'm sick of the ups and downs, you know, greatest guy on earth when the going's good and a son-of-a-bitch when I run through a yellow light. You grab the last thing of orange juice in Waldbaum's and somebody hates you for the next six hours . . . The wife wonders how the fuck she ever got mixed up with a prick like you when, in college, you were the guy whose smile used to make her cry herself to sleep. Just you *smiling* at her could do that, she wanted you so badly. So, you know, fuck it. "He was okay" sounds pretty damn good to me.

THE MERCY SEAT

ABBY Well, Ben, if it's any consolation . . . you're "okay" by me. I mean that. / More than okay.

BEN Thanks. / I appreciate that. *(He reaches over and kisses* ABBY *lightly on the cheek. A look between them, something almost soft, for a moment.)* Thanks. *(Beat.)* That's not what I meant before, anyway.

ABBY About what? / No . . .

BEN You know . . . / The "steel trap" thing.

ABBY Oh. Then what were you saying?

BEN I'm saying that . . . I don't know. I don't know what I'm saying exactly, but . . . not that.

ABBY Okay, good, just so long as it's clear as mud.

BEN I was never saying don't tell anyone. You know I wouldn't tell you that. I just . . . we had to be adult about this.

ABBY "Adult"?

BEN You know, grown-up. I mean . . .

ABBY I'm in my forties. I think that qualifies . . .

BEN I don't mean . . . Christ, you pounce on every word!

ABBY Well . . .

BEN I didn't not tell people because I was embarrassed or trying to lead two lives or whatnot . . . I was thinking of us. The overall situation.

ABBY Okay. If that's what it was, then okay.

BEN It was. We had to take it easy before, that's all.

ABBY I get it. All right.

BEN But now it's . . .

ABBY . . . fine. Right? Because you're *passed on.*

BEN Exactly . . . *(Almost a smile.)* I am.

ABBY You and the six thousand other . . . heroes.

BEN Come on.

ABBY Well, I'm sure a few of them are, anyway.

BEN Don't bring that up again, okay, not the . . .

ABBY What?

BEN The "hero" thing. I feel shitty enough.

ABBY Yeah? Really? *(Beat.)* I'm not sure you do. Not as shitty as
they feel, anyway.

BEN Who?

ABBY Whoever. The victims. Their families. No, I think you're
down the list a bit, Ben . . . *way* the heck down there.

BEN Abby, please, I mean . . . they're missing.

ABBY Dead.

BEN Whatever.

ABBY Exactly. Whatever. *(Beat.)* That's the position this puts me
in . . . six thousand people are dead, *killed*, some of them *our*
associates, and my entire response is "Oh well, whatever . . .
at least now we can sneak off to the *Bahamas." (Harsh
laugh.)* That's not very nice.

BEN I'm not . . . Who says you can't mourn? Huh?

ABBY Ben . . .

BEN I didn't say a word about that.

ABBY It's your whole demeanor about the . . .

BEN Go down and help sift debris if you want to, or keep a can-
dlelight vigil, I don't care . . . fuck! *(Beat.)* How did we even
get on this?

ABBY I think I accidentally started to feel something for a moment. Sorry.

BEN Come on, that's . . . bullshit. That's total . . .

ABBY Won't happen again. I promise.

BEN Fuck, Abby, that's unfair. *(Beat.)* I know a lot more people that work down there than you do. *Tons* more.

ABBY As in "tons" of rubble?

BEN STOP! Will you? God . . . *(Beat.)* I used to work out of that office, if you recall. I did. For years. And so, yeah, I got a bunch of faces in my head right now . . . Why the hell do you think I've been sitting here like a fucking pothead on the edge of the loveseat, staring into space for a day? Huh?

ABBY I don't know.

BEN Well, that's why.

ABBY Oh.

BEN All right? People I've talked to, had *coffee* with . . . I mean, all those guys from maintenance.

ABBY So . . . all this time you've been thinking about these people that you met down there over the years. Like, in the elevator, or at some little sandwich place . . . people like that?

BEN Of course!

ABBY Okay. *(Beat.)* I thought maybe you were thinking about us . . .

BEN No. I mean, yeah, I was, yes, but . . .

ABBY . . . and the family you're ditching . . . maybe all the hope they're probably pinning on the fact that you don't really work in that office anymore. I mean, the *prayers* they're sending out for you right now . . . I figured you were taking all *that* in! Shit, silly me.

BEN Abby . . . you just asked me how I . . .

ABBY Maybe you should've had one of the guys from *mainte-nance* bring you over some fucking cheese.

BEN That is so . . .

ABBY I'm serious!

BEN The guys from maintenance are probably all *dead!*

ABBY Oh, I'm sure some of them were cheating on their wives, you just need to call around!!

Suddenly ABBY's *buzzer rings. She and* BEN *freeze as it rings again. Before she goes to it,* BEN *gestures to her and she approaches the door. She hesitates, but goes out.* BEN *waits until she returns.*

ABBY It was my neighbor . . .

BEN Oh.

ABBY One floor down, actually.

BEN Okay.

ABBY She needs milk. For her kids.

BEN Ummm.

ABBY The stores are out. That's what she says.

BEN All right, so, we could, ahh . . .

ABBY Would you mind running up to the D'Agostinos? *(*BEN *looks at her, unsure how to take this.)* Kidding. I have the rest of that half gallon.

ABBY *grabs the milk out of the fridge and heads back to the door. Opens it and disappears for a moment.* BEN *stays hidden.*

ABBY Her husband works down there.

BEN He does?

ABBY Yes. I think so. I mean, I don't know *right* down there, but somewhere in the area.

BEN Oh. *(Beat.)* Did she say if . . . ?

ABBY No. And I didn't ask. She wanted milk and I gave it to her. *(Beat.)* Is that okay?

BEN Of course.

ABBY Good.

BEN I don't even like 2 percent . . .

ABBY *smirks at this and goes to the bathroom. Shuts the door. Water runs.* BEN *goes to a chair and sits. Plays with his phone. Turns it on. It rings almost immediately. He shuts it off and waits.* ABBY *reenters.*

ABBY What was that?

BEN What?

ABBY Just now. Did I hear your . . .

BEN What?

ABBY . . . phone?

BEN No.

ABBY I didn't?

BEN Uh-uh. I was, you know, fiddling with it, but it didn't ring. / I mean, the message thing went off, but . . .

ABBY Oh. / And who was it?

BEN I don't know. I didn't see . . . or check, I mean.

ABBY Not curious?

BEN No, I'll . . . I can find out later. / Check 'em at some other . . .

ABBY Sure. / Yep. *(Beat.)* Maybe when I go out to get you more cheese or something. When it's *safe*.

BEN Oh shit.

Neil LaBute

ABBY That'd be a good time to do it.

BEN Okay, I know that means something. Obviously that means something or you wouldn't have said it . . . so, go ahead.

ABBY I'm saying, pretty straightforwardly, that in the three years that we've been together I can't recall you taking a phone call or listening to a message in front of me. I can't. / Not a personal one, anyway.

BEN I have, too . . . / . . . That's not . . .

ABBY Yes, it is. It's completely true.

BEN No, I've . . . no.

ABBY Now, why do you think that is? *(Beat.)* Huh?

BEN Because I don't . . . / . . . maybe I didn't wanna hurt you.

ABBY What? / Hurt me? How?

BEN You know . . .

ABBY No.

BEN Make you listen in on that part of my life. The kids and, you know, the way we talk to each other, and all that kind of thing.

ABBY Oh.

BEN I've been . . . sparing you that.

ABBY Please . . .

BEN I have.

ABBY Well, don't, all right? Do me a favor . . . / I want the whole "you" or not at all.

BEN Fine. / What, you wanna hear every little . . . ?

ABBY No, not "every," just once! One time where you stand in front of me so I know what's coming out of your phone now is the same shit you're telling me ten minutes later.

BEN Oh God . . .

ABBY That'd be a real treat.

BEN I mean, you're just ranting here, seriously.

ABBY I am not ranting!

BEN Fuck, listen to yourself!

ABBY I can do ranting, believe me, I can, but this is not it . . . THIS IS NOT RANTING!

BEN All over a goddamn phone call.

ABBY It's not the call, Ben. It's not that.

BEN Then what?

ABBY It's trust! And openness! Your wanting to share everything with me . . . It's having the *desire* to do that! I'd probably listen to five minutes of your family drivel and pass out from boredom, but it's in the asking.

BEN I'm sorry . . . I didn't know.

ABBY And that's bullshit right there, that's what that is. It is because I've said this a thousand times, almost literally a thousand. No Secrets. / You can keep 'em from her but not from me, otherwise I might as well *be* her! Don't you get that?

BEN It's not a *secret* . . . / It's just a private phone call.

ABBY "Private" makes it secret! / I don't care!!

BEN With a *child*!! / But all I'm doing is . . .

ABBY Doesn't matter! It does not matter . . . because once you slip into the bathroom or turn on the fan or step back out onto the sidewalk, you might as well be . . . I dunno . . . Guy Burgess.

BEN Who?

ABBY Nothing . . . shit . . . it's not . . .

BEN The guy who wrote *Clockwork Orange?* / What the *hell* does he have to do with . . . ?

ABBY No . . . / That's Anthony Burgess! Your lit course didn't stick so good, did it?

BEN Well, I got the last name right, I just didn't . . .

ABBY Guy Burgess was a spy, an English spy who went over to the Soviets . . . he and some friends. In the fifties.

BEN Okay, I'm lost, but whatever . . .

ABBY Jesus, Ben, I'm saying it *still* applies if you're just reading to your daughters about *The Gingerbread Man!* You sneak off and make a call, always keep me out . . . the mind's gonna wander.

BEN I'm sorry. I thought it was the best thing.

ABBY Obviously.

BEN I did! I figured you didn't need to be constantly reminded of the situation.

ABBY I've never *known* what the situation was, because of the way you live your life!

BEN Why is it some federal thing if I wanna make a call in my . . . in the quiet of my own . . .

ABBY That's okay, *calling's* okay, but you can't . . .

BEN I'm a private person, so what?!

ABBY Well then, don't invite somebody in and ask them to hand over their life if you can't do the same fucking thing!

BEN Good God! And what "life" am I asking for, huh?

ABBY Ben . . .

BEN No, I mean it, let's not get completely off the . . .

ABBY Look at us!! Look at the current state of things and tell me I don't need to give up my life.

BEN Fuck, you are really on a tear, aren't you?! You really, *really* are.

ABBY Ben, what're we *actually* talking about here? You know, we keep dancing around it, but let's say it, let's just put the thing out there and see what we've got.

BEN Whatever. If you need to . . . go ahead.

ABBY All right. *(Beat.)* This "meal ticket" of ours . . . tell me what that is exactly.

BEN You know what it's . . .

ABBY Just say it. For me. / Please.

BEN This is stupid . . . / Fine. I'll . . . fine. *(Beat.)* I think that we can do it this time. / Be together.

ABBY Do what? / We *are* together.

BEN I mean always . . . as a couple.

ABBY You mean *run* away. Just say that's what . . .

BEN Not *run!* We don't have to . . . I mean, we can't even get out of town right now, so it's not exactly running.

ABBY You know what I mean.

BEN Yeah. *(Beat.)* Okay, so, yes, leave. Escape. Get away from this city and be with each other for the rest of our lives.

ABBY Or, as they used to call it . . . "run."

BEN Yeah. We could run.

ABBY Good. You said it. Just so it's been said.

BEN Don't you want to?

ABBY More than anything . . . / Since the day I met you.

BEN So do I! / Well, now we can.

ABBY We could've before. *Any* day before this, we could have.

BEN But now we can do it clean, you know, without any kind of hassle or . . . strings on us.

ABBY Was that the problem? Strings?

BEN Of course! Jesus . . . my wife, a fucking *mortgage* . . . All the shit that would've killed us, this thing we have.

ABBY A mortgage would've "killed" us?

BEN No, but . . . I just mean that . . .

ABBY We've lied to everyone we know, every minute of our time together for this long . . . because of a fucking *house payment*? Tell me that's not true.

BEN She would've buried me in a divorce, you know that!

ABBY So what? I would've uncovered you.

BEN No, no . . . I don't want that.

ABBY What, then, Ben? *What* do you want?

BEN You. I've told you that.

ABBY Just so long as you don't have to make a scene.

BEN No, but I . . . no.

ABBY As long as it could be done without causing a stink. Without you having to *sully* yourself.

BEN That's not what I'm . . .

ABBY Tell the truth, Ben!

BEN Maybe I was thinking about my kids! Okay?! / I'm not using them!

ABBY No, don't use them to . . . / Don't do that!

BEN You don't know what it's like, to see their faces . . . To, to imagine them *waiting* and . . . '

ABBY No, I don't, but . . .

BEN You have no fucking IDEA!

ABBY Ben, I know I don't, but I still . . .

BEN Maybe if you'd stop for a second, quit chewing your way up the corporate rungs there like a plague of fucking *locusts* and *have* yourself one . . . then, just possibly, you'll know!! / . . . Okay, then.

ABBY *starts to retort, but just shakes her head, turns away.* BEN *doesn't pursue her on this, having said more than he wished to.*

ABBY All right. / I accept that. *(Beat.)* 'S that true?

BEN What?

ABBY That you were protecting them? Is it? Tell me.

BEN *thinks for a moment before he speaks. He catches himself once before saying anything.* ABBY *studies him.*

BEN No, not completely. Or her . . . or you or anybody else.

ABBY Careful, Ben, I'm smelling a waft of truth over here.

BEN It's true. *(Beat.)* I was protecting me . . . How's that?

ABBY I like that just fine.

BEN Yeah?

ABBY If you're going to come clean, I like it a lot.

BEN I wanted this to work out, I did. For *every*body, yes, but most of all . . . for me. *(Beat.)* There, better? Clean . . .

ABBY We could've worked anything out. At any point.

BEN No, we couldn't . . . I don't think we could.

ABBY Why?

BEN Because I wasn't strong enough. *(Beat.)* But now I am. / I mean it, now I'm . . . ready.

ABBY Yeah? / You're sure?

BEN So totally sure . . .

ABBY .'Kay. *(Beat.)* I'm glad.

BEN Me too.

ABBY And what you're asking—I'm just saying it so that there's no question what we're up to here—what you want is for us to hide out in my house until it's safe, right? I mean, till the city gets itself back in gear, and then we would . . .

BEN Just, like, until the roads are open, you know, until we can drive ourselves out of . . .

ABBY Right, right, that's what I mean . . . stay here until we can get in the Saab and take off. Drive to another state, an airport somewhere, and slip away . . . while everybody else—not just your family, but friends, the company—all the people around you, really, can have this just *major* outpouring of grief in your honor . . . something like that?

BEN Yeah. That's the *Reader's Digest* version, but yes.

ABBY Okay, that's what I thought.

BEN It's soooo easy . . . really.

ABBY And my job—I should just, what? Call in with a *migraine* for a few weeks, or . . . ?

BEN I think so. I mean, otherwise you're giving up a lot of sick days. But if you use those first, then you can . . .

ABBY Eventually, though, once I do the whole "I'm too devastated to come back to work" thing, then what?

BEN You quit, right? Isn't that what we . . . ?

ABBY I quit. Just up and resign.

BEN It's what we already discussed. Last night.

ABBY I know, I guess I just never really heard the whole thing before, not laid out like this. *(Beat.)* So, I give up my position . . .

BEN Yes. I think a transfer's "iffy," I do . . . *(Beat.)* But you can take a similar position with another company—you were con-

sidering that place in Flagstaff, like, what, a year ago?—and
we set up house. I get myself a license, a credit card or two,
the whole deal. *(Beat.)* Get back into *sales*, even. Shit, I don't
care, whatever it takes.

ABBY Like the Witness Protection Program, or something.
Right?

BEN Sorta. You can even pick out my new name . . .

ABBY Huh. *(Beat.)* And my seniority with work now? My pension
plan and all the things I've worked toward, I should just . . .

BEN I know, Abby, I'm aware of the cost here . . . We're both giving up a lot.

ABBY What're you giving up again? Just remind me.

BEN My family! Shit, I mean . . .

ABBY I thought you wanted to give them up.

BEN I do, I do want to, but . . . not the girls. Not that. / Because! Jesus, I want to get out of all the other . . . you
know . . .

ABBY Then why do it? / Ahh, yes, the "other" stuff . . .

BEN *sits up at this, eager to make his point.* ABBY *watches him.*

BEN You think I *like* the idea of those little girls growing up without a father? Huh?! Well, I don't . . . but it's a hell of a lot better this way, letting 'em think whatever happened, okay,
rather than dragging them through court for a year and fight-
ing over who gets which *Barbie*, and for how long, and at
which designated location! *(Beat.)* This is better . . . as hard
and horrible as it's gonna be, it's still better.

Neil LaBute

ABBY You'll never be able to see them. You understand that, don't you? Not *ever* again.

BEN Yes.

ABBY No Disney, no proms, no walking down the aisle . . .

BEN I GET IT! Fuck . . . you think I didn't consider all that? Weigh it in? / Well, I did.

ABBY I'm just saying . . . / All right, then. Okay. *(Beat.)* Plus, you die a hero . . . right?

BEN Shit, Abby, that's not fair! Fuck!! *(Beat.)* It is the best thing for all of us . . . / YES! And it fell right in our laps.

ABBY You're sure? / I know, but . . .

BEN It absolutely is! This way we completely dodge around all the shit that I'd have to wade through . . . all the, you know.

ABBY Yeah, that messy shit, like . . . sitting your wife down and telling her honestly what you want. Shit like that?

BEN Fuck, fine . . . If this is gonna turn into one of your . . .

ABBY I'm just asking! Is that what it basically comes down to? I can cash in my life and go on the *lam* with you—because this is basically illegal, fyi, it is—I do that for you just so you can miss out on the discomfort of having to break it to your one-time *prom queen* that she doesn't turn you on anymore?

BEN Yes. / I'm asking you to do that.

ABBY Okay. / Just so we've said it.

BEN That's what I'm asking for.

ABBY Just so *truth* reared its ugly head here one time today.

BEN I am begging you to walk away . . . to leave a job that I've heard you bitch and moan about for the three years we've been together. To just pick up and leave this *co-op* that you

tell me you hate 'cause it's in the wrong section of town now
. . . I'm asking you to show me you love me by dumping the
lifestyle that I hear you crying about at, like, 2:30 in the
morning, when I'm lucky enough to be around you at 2:30 in
the morning, which is maybe *once* a month! I am asking you
to throw this mediocre, less than desirable single life of yours
out the fucking window and make a dash for the border with
me. *(Beat.)* Do it, Abby . . . we can do this.

ABBY I know we *can. (Beat.)* And do you love me?

BEN Abby . . . of course. You know that, I . . . yeah.

ABBY That's really not the same as just saying it.

BEN I do! Abby, please . . .

ABBY Then say it.

BEN Shit . . . I love you. There.

ABBY Wow, that makes me feel all tingly inside . . . / . . . and I
didn't even have to use the *bamboo shoots* . . .

BEN Come on . . . / . . . don't make this some . . .

ABBY Well, it didn't exactly *flow* out of you!

BEN *is suddenly up and crosses to* ABBY. *He takes her into
his arms and holds her. She starts to resist, but he is too
strong. She slowly melts into a hug that leads to a hun-
gry, naked kiss. She begins to cry. A long silence between
them.*

BEN . . . I do. Love you. Better?

ABBY Much.

BEN Good.'

ABBY Very.

Neil LaBute

BEN I agree. And that's what all this is about.

ABBY What?

BEN Making things very good. For us. *(A smile, finally, between them.* BEN *gives* ABBY *a last little squeeze and then moves away, dusting his clothes off and heading toward the bathroom door.)* I think I'm gonna take a shower, and then we can start to . . .

ABBY Ben.

BEN Yeah?

ABBY Let me ask you something.

BEN What, honey?

ABBY Just a theoretical thing, so don't get all . . .

BEN No, go ahead. What?

ABBY You're asking me to do this . . . all these things, for us.

BEN Yeah.

ABBY I'm just . . . Would you do the same for me?

BEN What do you mean?

ABBY In *theory,* would you make the same kind of gesture for me. If I asked you.

BEN Of course. Yes.

ABBY Even though you couldn't do it before this.

BEN We've talked about that . . . / It's different now.

ABBY I know, but . . . / That's what I'm saying. Now you've pulled your, you know, *Lazarus* thing . . . would you do it for me?

BEN Obviously, yeah . . . I'd do anything for you.

ABBY Anything?

BEN Yes, Abby, I would. *(Beat.)* Why're you so . . . ?

ABBY Then make the call.

BEN *stops with the door half open. Turns slowly to face* ABBY. *She doesn't waver.*

BEN What?

ABBY The call you were going to make. Yesterday, before all this.

BEN Huh?

ABBY I cannot do this. This "ride the rails" thing with you. *(Beat.)* If we're going to make it, you and me, I mean . . . then you need to call your wife and kids and let them know what's going on. Tell them the truth.

BEN Oh. So . . . this was all a . . . what, trick? Some kind of . . .

ABBY No, not a *trick*. I just can't . . .

BEN Get me to go out on a limb for you and then push me off the fucking branch?!

ABBY I'm just saying I can't do what you're asking me!

BEN Fine . . . fuck, fine, we'll just . . .

ABBY I don't wanna carry all that shit around, I'm not willing to do that!!

BEN Shit, SHIT! Shit on you for doing this.

ABBY I'm not "doing" anything, Ben, I'm asking you to.

BEN You know I can't! I cannot do that!! / No, no, NO!!

ABBY Why?! / WHY NOT?!!

BEN Because it ruins it. It ruins the ending.

ABBY *takes this in, processing.* BEN *fiddles with the door.*

ABBY This is not a movie, Ben.

BEN I'm not saying that.

ABBY You can't dictate how life is supposed to . . .

BEN Yeah, I could . . . In this *one* instance, I could've! *(Beat.)* We had no chance here . . . A day ago, we were just another two people fucking each other and pretending that we had something special. Now we've got a chance to actually make it that. Special . . .

ABBY It wasn't special?

BEN It was an *affair*, Abby, fuck, can't we just be . . . ?

ABBY It was special to me.

BEN Of course it was "special," that's the wrong word. I just mean that it was common, regular. It happens. But this thing . . . this disaster . . . makes what we're doing . . . possible.

ABBY I see . . . Now I see.

BEN All we have to do is walk away, Abby! Not run . . . just walk. Walk off into the sunset.

ABBY All right. Okay. Duly noted. *(Beat.)* But after you make the call.

BEN Shit . . . Abby . . . / Don't ask me to . . .

ABBY I *need* you to do that for me. / Will you? Ben?

BEN I can't . . . / . . . oh God . . .

ABBY Please . . . / Ben, please . . . for me . . . *Please*.

BEN Yes. *(Beat.)* Okay.

ABBY Thank you.

BEN I will. *(Beat.)* You, umm, you want me to . . . what, make the call that I was gonna make yesterday, right? The call I said I was going to make before this . . . all this . . . happened.

ABBY That's what I want. Yes.

BEN All right, Abby, I'll do that.

BEN *crosses back to the couch and sits, rubbing his eyes. Pulls his cell phone out of his pocket and switches it on.* ABBY *starts across the room.*

ABBY I'll give you your privacy.

BEN No, you don't have to.

ABBY It's okay, you should have time to . . . / It's fine.

BEN I want you to hear this, Abby. / ABBY! *(*ABBY *stops and looks at him.)* You need to hear this . . . Go ahead, take a seat.

ABBY *crosses back toward the kitchen and sits on the edge of a stool near the counter.* BEN *takes a deep breath, then dials a number and waits. After a moment, Abby's phone begins to ring. She looks up, startled, and mimes to* BEN*: "What should I do?" She starts to panic, but* BEN *motions for her to take the call.*

ABBY Hello?

BEN Hi.

ABBY Ben? Why're you . . . ?

BEN Just listen. Okay? Just . . . listen to me. *(Beat.)* So . . . this was the call I was going to make yesterday.

ABBY No, no, I don't want you to *pretend* with me, I want you to call them and . . .

BEN Abby, shut the fuck up and listen! I was going to call *you* yesterday, not them. I was gonna make this call on my way to work, and then I thought, What the hell, it's only a few blocks over, I'll stop in and talk to her. Tell her face-to-face. Be brave, like she's always asking me to be . . . she deserves that. *(Beat.)* I wasn't gonna phone home, Abby, I can't do that. You can call my wife, spill your guts if you want to, but I'll never be able to . . . can't do that. *(Beat.)* That's why all . . . *this* . . . suddenly seemed so logical, like the only thing possible. And I wanted it. God, I did! But now . . . Look, I think you're great, and we've had, umm, the most amazing . . .

ABBY Ben . . . don't.

BEN No, I promised you I'd make a call, and this is it. I'm calling to tell you I can't do this anymore, I'm tired of dodging and hiding and all the, just, bad shit I've done so effortlessly since we met. If you'd taken this . . . meal ticket . . . of ours, then great. I'd've worked in a fucking *lumberyard* the rest of my days to be with you, but if you wanna make me come clean about what I've done, purge all my sins for some un-fucking-fathomable reason . . . I mean, if I'm publicly forced to choose between those little girls' hearts and your *thighs*, well then, there's just not much question. *(Beat.)* Sorry, Abby, I'm really very . . . I don't know. Just sorry. G'bye.

BEN *clicks off the call. After a moment, his cell phone begins ringing and continues while they sit staring at each other.* ABBY *slowly hangs up.* BEN *finally snaps his phone shut.*

ABBY Goodbye. *(Beat.)* So . . . you were never going to call your . . . ? And my little "pick-me-up," to encourage you, that was . . . ? Hmm, what? A last suck for good luck? *(She slowly goes over to her things and begins to suit up. Coat, hat, scarf, etc.)*

BEN What're you doing?

ABBY Going to get some more cheese . . . Kidding. I'll go to work, I guess. I'm gonna walk over to our office and find out what's happened up there . . . see if I can . . . something . . . Just tell me the company line before I go. Are you gonna stick with the "hero" thing . . . went up in the fire and all that, or are you gonna miraculously wake up in some alley and stagger back to your desk tomorrow? We should get our stories straight.

BEN I don't . . . know . . . I don't know what to . . . do.

ABBY You call your family, or you don't. You run for the hills, or you don't. You come back in and work on the AmTel account with us or not. Your life's in front of you right now, Ben . . . but *you* have to choose. *(Beat.)* You already made one choice— me—so you can leave the keys on the counter or in your *ficus tree* or wherever . . . and if I see you back at work, that'll be great. It will be. *(She moves toward the door, but hesitates.)* Look, you can't stay here. Uh-uh. I'm not gonna rat you out, whatever you decide, I won't do that. I'll show you some mercy . . . more than you've ever shown me, anyway. But I'm not gonna give you any cash or maps or, you know, *waterproof matches.* I'm not Harriet Tubman and I just don't feel like helping. So, you'll have to do whatever—you can't use your ATM card out there or any of that other shit, either, I mean, not if you really wanna disappear—but if you're going to start over, then do it. Right now. Today. *(Beat.)* Otherwise, wash your face and go home. See your children, tell them you love them. Tell your wife, too. Because you do, you know. Love

her. You must, or you'd already be at that lumberyard in the
Bahamas . . . with me.

BEN Abby, I'm not . . . It's only because I'm . . . I'm just a little
lost right now.

ABBY Yeah, me too, Ben. *(ABBY pulls her scarf up around her
mouth and opens the front door. Rattles her keys.)* I am, too.

BEN Couldn't we just . . . ?

*ABBY closes the door behind her, and the lock slides shut, cut-
ting BEN off in mid-sentence. A kind of quiet falls over the room.
After a long moment, BEN sits back on the couch and pulls his
cell phone out of his pocket, turning it on. It rings almost immediately. BEN stares at it, turning it over in his hands. It rings and
rings.*

Silence. Darkness.